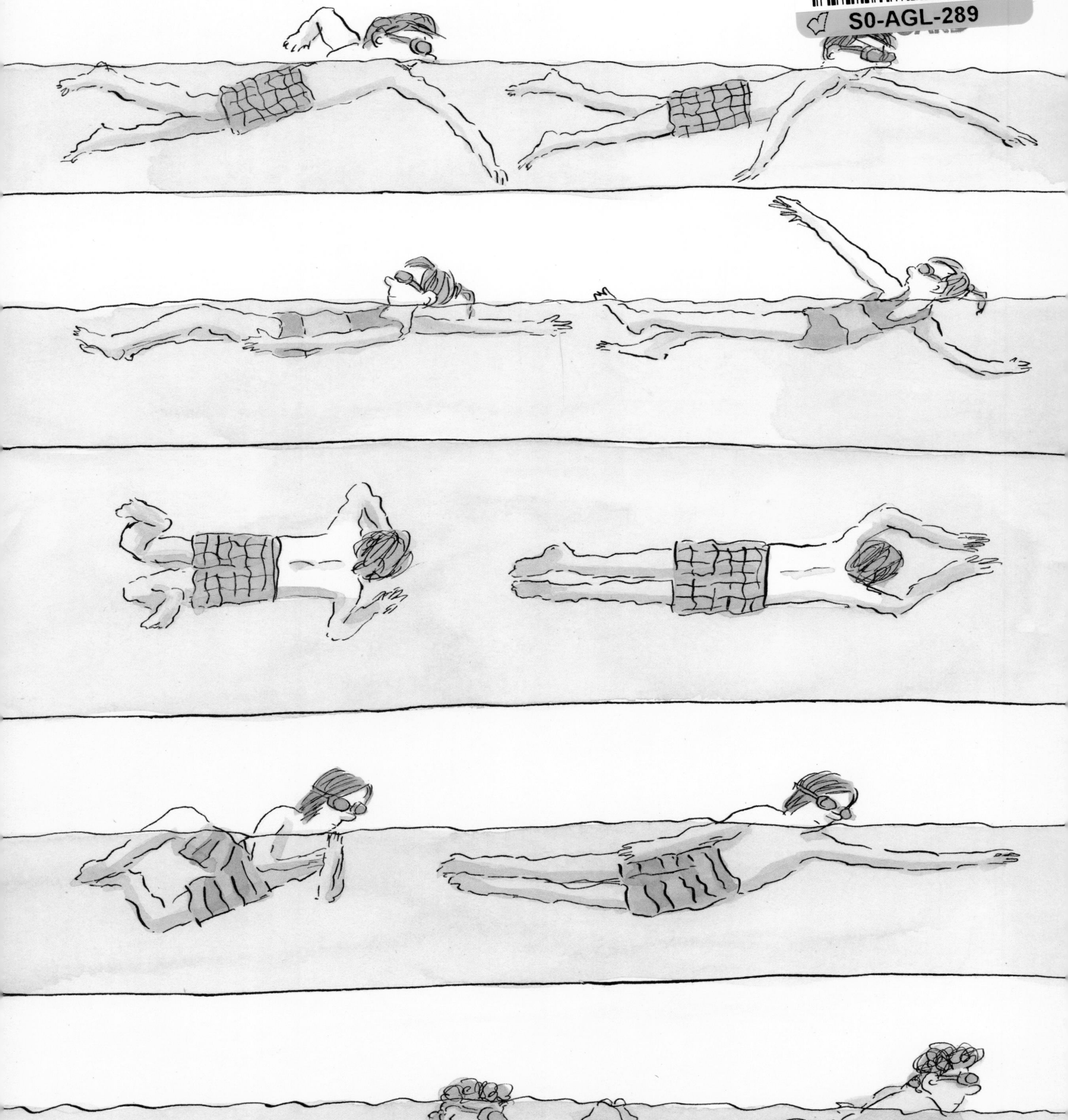

SWIMMING, SWIMMING

GARY CLEMENT

GROUNDWOOD BOOKS
HOUSE OF ANANSI PRESS
TORONTO BERKELEY

FISHY
FOOD

FISHY
OOD

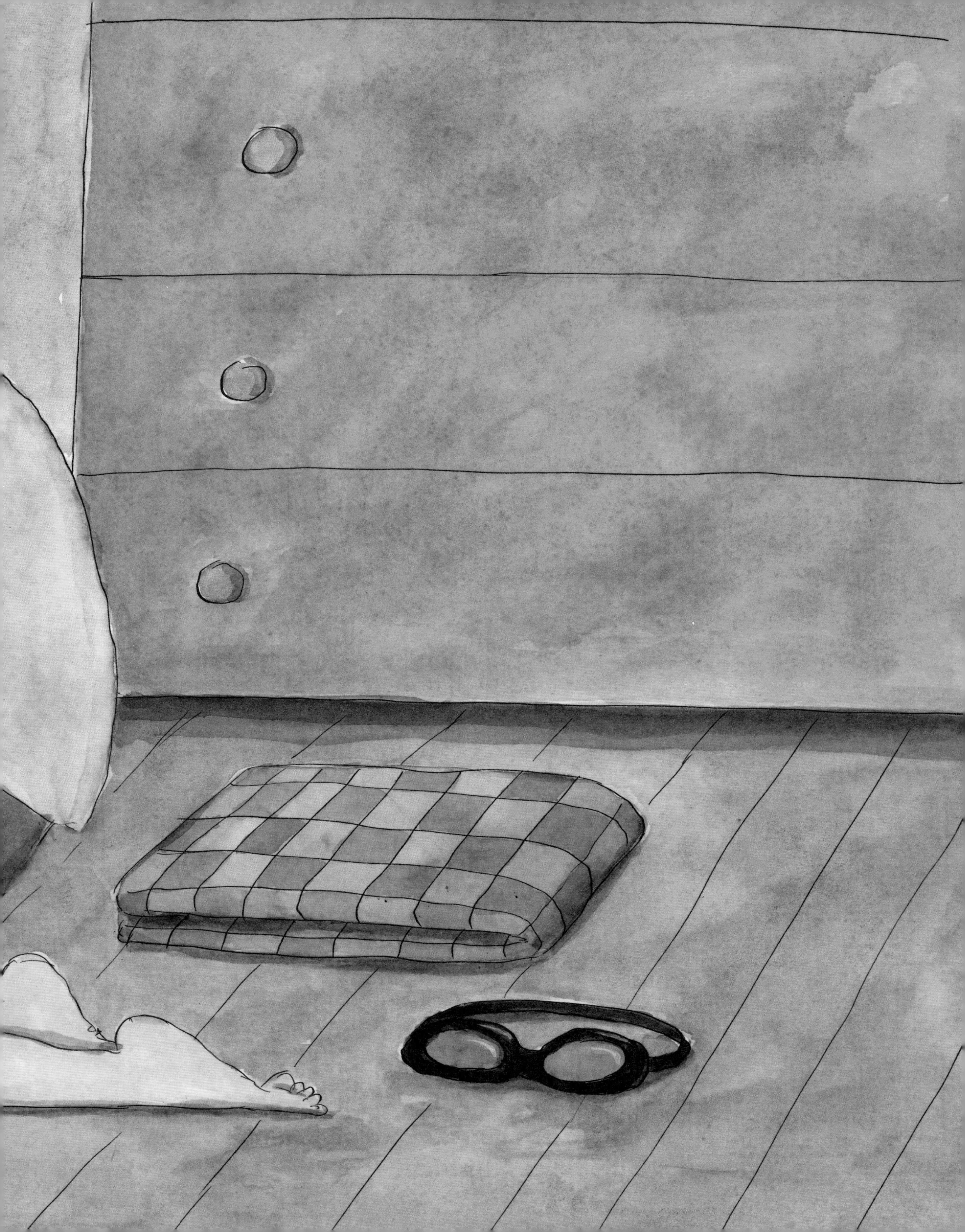

COMMUNITY POOL
843

SHOWERS

BOYS
LOW END

GIRLS
HS

SWIMMING,

SWIMMING

IN
SWIM
PO

A
MING
OL.
GIRLS
VHS

WHEN DAYS ARE HOT

WHEN DAYS ARE COLD

IN
A

SWIMMING
POOL.
SPF 45

BREAST

STROKE

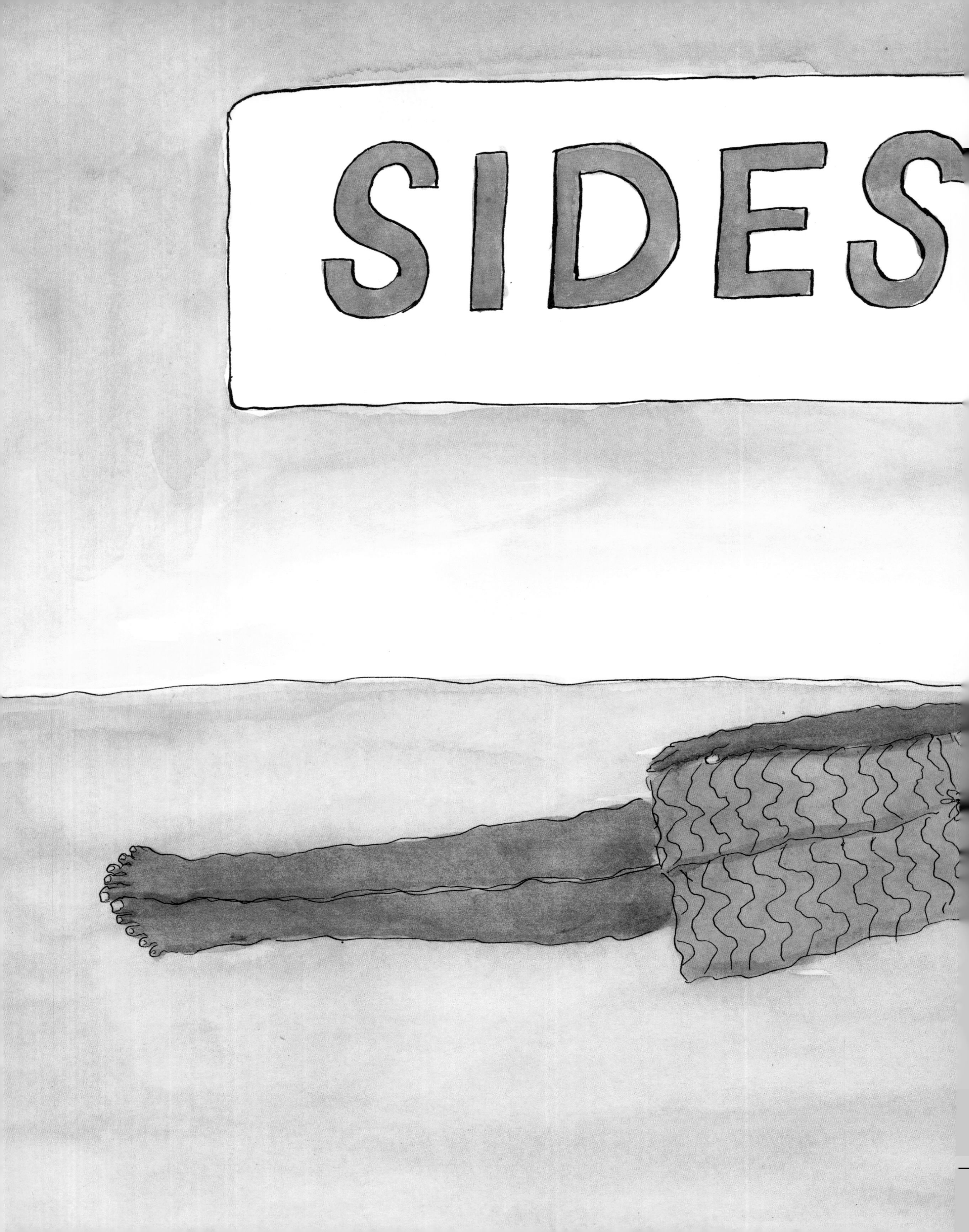
SIDES

TROKE

FANCY DIVING TOO!

OH DON'T NEVER HAD ELSE TO

YOU WISH YOU
ANYTHING
DO?

BOYS

GIRLS

SHOWERS

Mister Ice Cream

COMMUNITY POOL
843